The Secret Dragons

Written and Illustrated

by

Fran Stoval

All the places in this book and historical people are real. The characters and events in this book are imaginary.

ISBN 9781076379313

Printed by Amazon

Acknowledgments

Thank you to each of these people who at one time or another encouraged and inspired me to write this book.

Heidi Almen
Mary Ellen Bdzil
Sandy Charles – Published Author
James Chamberland
Carrie Connolly
Jaida Connolly
Louise Hassman
Rich Hassman
Paula Jaramillo
Annie Kuiper – Editor Extraordinaire
Donny Langan
Marion Langan
Amanda Leibee
Cienna Muller
Kaley Muller
Laila Muller
Heather McClenahan – Los Alamos Historical Society
        Former Executive Director
Patrick Rutherford
Warren Sevander
Sharon Snyder – Bathtub Row Press
        Publications Director
Chase Stovall
Devan Stovall
Jeff Stovall
Leonard Stovall
Riley Stovall
Stacey Stovall

Author's Note

In the high deserts of northern New Mexico, you will find a mountain range; they are like an enchanted forest. The Indians call them the "Jemez," and they hold many secrets. Some of these secrets are known, but I am telling you a new secret that must stay between the pages of this book.

The places you will read about are real. The people are real, and for sure, the dragons are real. But, you know if the word gets out, the dragons might have to move to a safer place. We don't want that!

I want you to go up in these mountains, close your eyes and feel their presence. Come along with me, and take an adventure with Emily, Mark, Clare and of course Bow . . . a very colorful dragon. Come along, learn a little history, and join in the adventures of the newest guardian dragon!

Fran Stoval
www.franstoval.com

Table of Contents

Illustrations

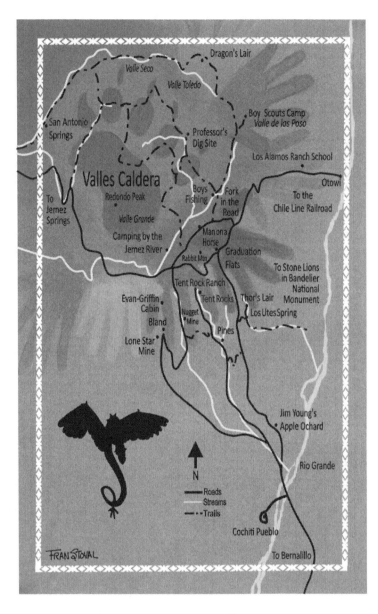

Dragons Eye View

Chapter 1
Tent Rock Guest Ranch
1937

The Dawsons are on their way to the Tent Rock Guest Ranch.[1] Twelve-year-old Emily and Pepper, the family dog, are nestled together in the open **rumble seat** of the family's Model A Ford **roadster**. Her mom, Delores, is driving and Pilar, a Cochiti **Pueblo**[2] **Indian**, is in the passenger seat. Emily's dad, John, and her sixteen-year-old brother Mark are in the Model A Ford truck following close behind. The truck is loaded with supplies for running the Tent Rock Guest Ranch. They are on the last leg of their journey.

The vehicles pass through a narrow part of the canyon, so Emily gets a close up look at her surroundings. The tarnished tan walls of the high cliffs loom up on both sides of the canyon, sometimes only 20 feet apart. They repeatedly cross the Rio Chiquito, a stream that has found its way from the hot springs in the Jemez Mountains of northern New Mexico. The sides of the road are dressed with birch trees; they grow tall trying to reach the sun. As the Dawson family drives through this narrow spot of the canyon, the trees create an **arbor** effect, and the sun punches through the leaves leaving bright splashes of light on the ground. Close to the edge of the stream, flowers are blooming. The walls stretch apart forming a large clearing. The Dawsons find themselves in the ghost town of Pines. Still standing is the centerpiece of the town, the old sawmill. The mill ran only for a few years during the gold rush era.

The canyon splits in two and they take the Pines Canyon road that forks to the left. Immediately on the right, the giant **tent rocks** jump into sight. As they get closer, the rocks hover over them like giant statues. Now the Tent Rock Guest Ranch is just minutes away.

Emily gets a close up look.

3

Emily's thoughts turn inward to the preparations it took to get them to this day.

This is the second year Emily's parents have managed the Tent Rock Guest Ranch. People come from all over the country to experience this mountain adventure. The guests rest, ride horses and have many outdoor activities like archery, nature walks, hiking, and fishing in the large pond.

The Guest Ranch is located at the south end of the Valles **Caldera**,[3] a volcano that blew it's top 1.15 million years ago. Millions of years of erosion formed mesas, canyons, and huge rock formations called tent rocks. These creations look like cones. They are made of a soft **pumice** rock and have a large hard rock that sits on top like a cap.

In the late eighteen hundreds, people came to this area to search for gold, silver, and **opals** in these mountains.

In the next canyon over, is the town of Bland,[4] the largest of the mining towns in the mining district. When Emily and Mark's dad was younger, he went to Bland and mined for gold and silver, but that didn't pan out. He moved to

Bernalillo, a small farming community outside of Albuquerque, New Mexico. The best thing that happened to him was meeting and falling in love with Dolores Gonzales, their mom.

Leaving their home early that morning they reached their first stop, the Bernalillo Mercantile Company.[5] The Seligman family owns the "Merc," as everyone calls it; a large grocery and hardware store where miners, ranchers, and lumbermen buy supplies and is a source of information about the area.

Emily and Mark watched as their dad and Mr. Seligman stacked the truck as high as they dared with items they would need to run the Guest Ranch.

Next, they headed north about 21 miles to Cochiti Pueblo, located on the west side of the Rio Grande. They stopped and picked up Pilar who helps their mom with the everyday tasks of running the Guest Ranch. Just thinking about Pilar's cooking starts Emily's mouthwatering. She makes the best-baked bread in an horno, a large round adobe oven that sits in the front yard.

Pilar is waiting for them by the horno.

The vehicles entered the dusty **plaza** of the pueblo. Many people had come out to greet them. Pilar was waiting for them by the horno. She was dressed in traditional Cochiti clothes, a bright colored dress, **squash blossom necklace** of turquoise stones and silver and legging **moccasins** on her feet. Pilar's family fed them a wonderful lunch of green chili stew and freshly made bread. They were so full that it was hard to climb back in the vehicles and move on.

Their next stop was Young's Apple **Orchard,**[6] located at the mouth of Cochiti Canyon. When they arrived at the orchard, they piled out of the vehicles. John headed to the apple shed to stop and chat with Jim who was just getting his apple orchard up and running. He grows red and golden delicious apples. The trees were all in bloom. Emily and Pepper ran out under the trees as the breeze throws the blossoms down on them like snow. Jim helped them load up some of last fall's apple crop.

They were back on the dirt road, and as they got closer to the tent rocks, Emily closed her eyes and envisioned the camping trip she, Mark and their friend Clare had taken to Graduation

Flats last summer. They were snuggled up in their bedrolls watching the full moon move across the sky one night when they first heard some chattering sounds coming from the horizon. They all looked up at the moon and had been surprised by seeing snake-like creatures with wings crossing the sky. They were convinced they had seen seven dragons[7] that night. With any luck, Emily was hoping they would see them again this year.

Just then the roadster hit a large bump and Emily's mind bounced back to the present. She could see from the rumble seat that they were just a matter of minutes from their summer home, the Tent Rock Guest Ranch.

She was thinking . . . let the summer adventures begin!

Chapter 2
We're Here!

We're here! We're here! The vehicles stop; the doors fly open. Emily and Pepper jump out of the car and hop around like a couple of grasshoppers. It feels like they had been in the vehicles for years. After they stretch out their arms and legs, they are ready to go.

Mom speaks up, "Now Emily and Mark don't go too far. We have a lot of unpacking to do."

"Yes mom," Emily answers, "I'm just going over to the barn to see Ah-zaah, Toco, and Chili."

Mark, standing next to the truck, shakes the dust from his Stetson hat. Mark is a Boy Scout[8] in the northern New Mexico Council, in Bernalillo, and recently turned 16. Last winter he earned his Eagle Scout award, the highest rank in the Scouting program.

He looks nothing like his blond-hair, blue-eyed sister Emily who favors her dad's English **heritage**. Mark's face is a warm honey color; his eyes are jet black; he is small, sturdily built and looks Spanish, like his mom.

Mark also replies, "Sure, mom. I'll start helping dad unload the supplies."

Emily grabs an apple for Chili, her horse at the Ranch, and heads toward the barn. She thinks about Ah-zaah, whose name means Prairie Wolf. He is an **Apache Indian** who lives at the Guest Ranch all year round. He is an excellent horseman because his tribe was **nomadic,** living on the plains where they followed and hunted millions of **buffalo**. He is a slender man. He does not look anything like the **Pueblo Indians.** He has more pointed features and deep, piercing blue eyes. His skin is very brown and looks like shoe leather. He always has a red bandana wrapped around his head.

Toco sits pompously on Ah-zaah's arm.

Last year Ah-zaah told them he was a **shaman**, which means spiritual leader. In the evening's last summer, when the kids sat around the campfire, he told stories about his tribe and his people. Everyone loves listening to him. Their favorite stories were about the dragons that live in the Jemez Mountains and how they moved there from the southern plains because the "white man" had killed off their food source, the buffalo.

Emily spots Ah-zaah. He has a large black raven[9] named Toco sitting pompously on his arm. Emily puts her finger out to Toco. He wraps his beak around it and moves his head up and down in a handshaking ritual. Ah-zaah greets her in the Apache language "taná a nė see?" which means, "How are you?"

Emily says she is fine, and then asks Ah-zaah, "How is Chili? When can I ride her?" He points to her on the far side of the corral. Emily pulls out the apple she has in her jacket pocket and runs up to Chili calling her name. The horse looks up at her. Emily sees that she recognizes her and the horse starts prancing. Chili is a beautiful **appaloosa**, mostly gray with black leopard spots. Emily pats Chili's forehead as the horse munches down the apple. Emily looks back to the ranch complex and sees the nine cabins that need to be prepared for the arriving guests and the truck and car that need unloading.

"I have to go," Emily, utters she looks back at Chili. "I promise you Chili, I'll return as soon as I can, but now I need to help with the unpacking."

After dinner, the family sits around a large dining table to have a meeting about who will be their guests.

Mom starts, "We have three days before our first guests arrive. That will be the Johnson family. Let's put them in the Lupine cabin. (All the cabins have different flower names.) Next to come will be the Smiths the following day."

Emily jumps up and squeals, "Yippee, Clare is coming!"

The Smiths were at the Guest Ranch last summer. Clare and Emily are both twelve years old. They had become best friends and had been pen pals over the past year. The Smiths live in Washington DC. Clare had **polio** when she was younger so she must wear braces on her legs, but she gets around very well. Mom explained last year that polio attacks the nervous system and can cause the muscles to develop abnormally. Polio affected Clare's legs, so her leg muscles are weak and she ended up having to wear braces to help her walk.

"Over the next week we will have all the cabins filled," dad says. "Most people were here last summer, but there is one new guest you need to be aware of . . . Professor Harold P. Shuttlebutt. He's a **paleontologist**."

"A WHAT?" Emily asks.

Mark answers, "A paleontologist. They study old bones that have turned into rocks which are called **fossils**."

Dad tells the kids, "He will be going out on pack trips into the Valles Caldera for days at a time. He is looking for dinosaur fossils. The Guest Ranch will be his base camp."

Mom adds, "Come on everyone, let's get these dishes done. We have a busy three days ahead of us."

Chapter 3
Summer Guests

Cleaning, washing, making beds, and just a mess of things to do consume the next three days. Emily and Mark can hardly wait until the load will lighten up so they can go horseback riding with Clare, and explore the surrounding area.

Last year when they were checking out Spruce Canyon, Mark found a **dagger**. It looked very old. He had shown it to Ah-zaah, who thought it might be Spanish. Mark made a sheath for it so he could carry it on his belt, and now he carries it wherever he goes.

Seeing Mark over at the barn, Emily grabs an apple for Chili and heads that way. As she approaches, she sees Ah-zaah teaching Mark the raven word for untying. Emily knows a few phrases but Mark has mastered 30 or more so he can talk to Toco like Ah-zaah does. Ravens are one of the smartest birds around. They make click and clack sounds, which are like images for things they see. Toco is sitting on a fence railing. Mark makes a couple of clicking sounds. Toco jumps to the ground and goes to a rope tied to the fence post. Watching him is fun as he struts up to the rope, examines it, turns his head from one side to the other and then begins pulling the knot apart. It doesn't take him long. Then he flies back up to the fence railing and makes a bunch of "caw, caw" sounds. You can tell he is really proud of himself.

Emily greets Chili and holds out the apple to her. The horse sniffs the apple and soon has it munched down. Looking up, Emily sees a big cloud of dust over by the road indicating a vehicle is approaching. She runs back to the big house and sees a car pulling into the parking area. Sure enough, Clare and her parents have arrived. Clare is a tall, beautiful, freckled-faced girl with **carrot top** hair. You can see the braces on her legs, which make her walk stiffly, but she doesn't need crutches. Emily and Clare laugh and embrace each other. They are looking forward to spending time together again this summer.

"Emily," mom begins, "Will you show the Smiths to their cabin and help them with their bags?"

Then she reminds her, "Professor Shuttlebutt will also be arriving today, so please come right back to help."

Emily gets the Smiths settled into their cabin. Then a large black car comes roaring into the parking area. She and Clare hurry back to the parking area where they see her mom, dad, and Mark standing there ready to greet the new guests.

Driving the big black car is a small man. He jumps out, runs around to the passenger door, and holds it open for a large man.

The manservant is dressed in traditional black Chinese clothing. He has a long black ponytail that hangs down to his waist, a pencil-thin mustache that drapes down to his chin on both sides of his mouth, and he wears sandals.

Professor Shuttlebutt is a large pear-shaped man. He is balding, and his hair sticks out around the edges of his head like a ring of wild grass. The top of his head shines like a polished shoe. His feet are huge and his toes stick out like he is about to walk in two different directions.

Both of them circle back around the car to greet everyone. The Professor introduces himself and his manservant, Wong Way. They both look so out of place in this outdoor setting. Emily thinks, "What an odd pair."

Emily's dad offers to take the Professor and Wong Way to their cabin, and he and Mark help them with their luggage. What a **procession**! John carrying bags, then Mark, carrying more bags, next the Professor, and finally, Wong Way trailing several paces behind the Professor taking small fast baby steps to keep up with everyone. The girls just stand and watch, covering their mouths, to hide their giggles, because the whole scene is just so comical. Mom turns and stares at them, giving them the LOOK . . . (you know the one you get when you had better stop doing what you are doing!)

"What an odd pair."

Chapter 4
Campfire Dragon Stories

It is now the middle of June, and all the cabins have guests in them. Everyone has been having all kinds of adventures. Of course, Emily and Clare like to ride their horses the best.

The Professor and Wong Way pack the mule and leave for a week, they say, to look for fossils in the Jemez. It is such a sight to see them ride out of the Guest Ranch. "Puffessor," the girls now call him, has no **"horse sense"** at all. Wong Way has a footstool that he takes with them. He sets it next to the horse to help the Puffessor get up in the saddle. Wong Way pulls a **pack mule** with their supplies behind the horses as they both head to Cochiti Mesa.

Every Friday evening, the Guest Ranch has a large fire in the fire pit. Everyone sings songs, roasts marshmallows, and sometimes Ah-zaah tells stories about his life on the plains. This Friday night, Emily, Mark, Clare, and Ah-zaah are the last sitting around the campfire. As they all gaze into the dying embers of the fire, while roasting marshmallows, Ah-zaah begins one of his tales.

"This is a special year in the world of the dragons. The oldest dragon is failing in health. He must be at least 250 years old, and now the dragons are waiting for the birth of a baby dragon that will become the new guardian dragon.

The dragons are moving around more and more; if you look up into the night sky, you may see them. They are waiting for the July full moon because that night the new king dragon will be born. Toco and I have seen signs that the moon is getting fuller and that this night is near. When the new dragon is born, there will be a great celebration. Dragons will come from all over, even as far away as Mexico to meet this new king."

Ah-zaah tells stories about his life.

"Please tell us more," Emily interjects. "Tell us again how the dragons ended up here in the Valles Caldera."

"OK little ones, I will tell you again," replies Ah-zaah. "Since the beginning of time, my people lived on the plains. We were nomads; we wandered from place to place. Our stories were passed down from generation to generation, always by a shaman, a very holy man. The shaman told me about the dragons that also lived on the plains at that time. The dragons were called **Amphitheres.** No one had seen these dragons for a long time. They were described to me as snake-like creatures with wings like a bird. Their wings had rainbow-colored feathers; they had golden bellies and scaly purple skin. They made a high-pitched squawk and traveled usually at night in small flocks. Their main source of food was buffalo.

The dragons moved to the Jemez Mountains when the white man brought the **Iron Horse** across the plains and killed their food source.

Many years ago, Toco and I found a dragon **lair** and we **staked it out**. Sure enough, a dragon appeared and I got my first look at a dragon. It was just as my ancestor had described it.

A few years later I met Effie Jinks,[10] a woman over in Bland, who owns the hotel. She told me she had befriended the dragons who now live in the Jemez Mountains. She knows where they live in the Valles Caldera area."

Toco started flapping his wings and making some clicking sounds. "OK Toco, I'll tell them," says Ah-zaah. "Dragons don't like to eat sheep, it gives them hairballs. They don't like to eat humans either. Humans leave a bad taste in their mouth for days."

Just then mom shows up and announces, "Sorry kids, it's time to go to bed. See you all in the morning." As the embers die down, everyone fades into the dark.

Chapter 5
Dragon Cave & Earthquake

The next morning Emily, Mark, and Clare decide to do some exploring on horseback. Toco keeps an eye on them, while he flies high above. He sees they are heading back down the canyon passing Pines. They find the Bland Frijoles trailhead, which takes them east towards **Bandelier National Monument**.[11] The three of them climb out of Cochiti Canyon and then stay on top of the flat mesa. The trail goes north along Saint Peter's Dome Road and then descends off the road onto Capulin Canyon trail. At the bottom of the canyon, they find the Los Utes Spring, which is a perfect place to have the burritos that Pilar had packed for them that morning before they left. Mark **hobbles** the horses to graze. Of course, you might know who shows up as soon as the food is laid out . . . who else but a bird who can really smell food miles away, Toco!

The mountain spring waterfall is refreshing, and everyone watches as the water dances down the rocks and into the stream. The talk turns to searching for some Indian **artifacts,** since ancient Indians once lived in this area, or maybe even trying to find some of the Indians' **petroglyphs**. Mark tells the girls, "There are some petroglyphs farther down in the canyon. They are close to the Rio Grande where there is a ceremonial place called '**Stone Lions**' that are still used by the Indians today."

Mark and Toco start carrying on some bird conversations.

Clare speaks up, "Mark, what's Toco saying?"

Mark answers, "Toco tells me this is the canyon where he and Ah-zaah had found the dragon lair. Toco wants to know if we would like to see it. He says the dragon no longer lives there."

Clare says eagerly, "That sounds like a lot more fun than seeing a bunch of old Indian rock carvings. Let's do that!"

The kids ride their horses up the canyon until they see Toco sitting on a large rock. They tie up the horses and move up the canyon to where Toco is waiting. In this part of the canyon, the walls are very steep on both sides. Then Toco caws like he is saying "this way." They climb a small hill but still don't see a cave. Toco flies up and over a rabbit bush and disappears. Sure enough, behind the bush is a small opening. The kids have to get on their hands and knees to get into the cave. Mark, the prepared one, has brought flashlights. He hands one to each of the girls. They all shine their lights in the cave. It opens up into a large room where everyone can stand up. The ceiling is black with soot. There are bones scattered all over the floor. The kids begin to examine the walls. They find something that looks like petroglyphs.

Clare notes, "The writing on the walls looks like **runes**, an ancient alphabet I learned about in school. Emily, do you have a pencil and some paper in your saddlebag? I'll copy the writing down."

Emily goes back to her horse and retrieves a pencil and some paper. Once Clare copies the writing down, she notices some gold dust on the dirt floor. Mark takes a sheet of paper and uses his dagger to scrape some of the gold dust onto it. He folds the paper to save the dust. The three of them go outside and look around for other signs of dragons. All they find are some **obsidian rocks** that the Indians used to make arrowheads. Emily reaches down, picks up a small rock, and sees that it's a blue opal. She shows it to Mark and Clare and then buries it in her pocket.

Realizing they had spent too much time at the spring and exploring the cave, they all agree to head back. The kids retrace their steps, mount up, and turn their horses back to the Guest Ranch. They are just starting to pass the tent rocks when it happens. The ground starts to move under them!

The horses nervously prance up and down and Mark yells, "'EARTHQUAKE!' Get off the horses! Pepper can chase them to the Ranch where Ah-zaah will corral them."

Get off the horses!

Mark then tells Toco to fly ahead and let Ah-zaah know the horses are coming. The horses run down the road with Pepper barking and chasing them. When the dust settles, the kids notice the earthquake has knocked down some rocks that are all over the road.

Mark tells the girls, "We need to move these rocks off the road."

As they push the rocks from the road, one rock stands out. It does not really look at all like a rock; it looks more like a very large ostrich egg that was covered with mud, but now most of the dried dirt has been knocked off. The rock has bright green markings. "WOW," they all say together as they are curious about the egg-shaped rock. Mark picks it up; he carefully wraps his jacket around it and places it into his **knapsack**. After moving the rest of the rocks off the road, the kids start walking back to the Guest Ranch.

Chapter 6
Dragon Egg

When the kids arrive back at the Guest Ranch, they see that everyone is fine, just a little shaken-up. There is some minor damage to the buildings. John saw the horses running into the parking area and he helped Ah-zaah get them into the corral. Toco told Ah-zaah about the kids so Ah-zaah relayed to the kids' parents that everyone was safe and that they were walking back from the tent rocks.

It is a happy reunion when the kids get back. Everyone sits down for supper except Mark.

He had gone ahead of Emily and Clare to the chicken coop, to hide the knapsack with the egg in it for safekeeping.

At the supper table, they are all talking at once about the earthquake, how the horses had reacted, and how they had cleaned up the rocks that had littered the road during all that shaking.

After supper, the kids meet outside and decide to go back to the chicken coop. They hold up what they thought was a rock but see it must be an egg. Mark puts a candle up to the egg to see if he can see anything inside. He does see faint traces of something inside the egg.

Mark wonders aloud, "It looks kind of like a snake."

"I think I see wings," Emily adds.

"Look!" Clare says, "I see something like a horn where its face is."

Too tired to do much more, Mark hides the egg under a large hen and they all make plans to come back in the morning to figure out what to do.

After chores the next morning, they meet back at the chicken coop. Mark has the gold dust, Emily has the blue opal and Clare has the paper with the runes copied on it. They get the egg from under the hen to examine it again. It is nice and warm.

Emily questions, "What do you think it is… a snake or a bird?"

"It kind of looks like both don't you think?" answers Clare. "Do you think it could be a dragon egg?"

Mark replies, "Maybe the best thing we can do is take it to Ah-zaah and see what he thinks."

Mark carefully puts the egg in his knapsack and the kids head over to the corral. They see Ah-zaah and Mark gets his attention and asks him to meet them behind the barn. Mark tells him about the cave that Toco had shown them and the things they had discovered. Next Mark tells him what happened after the earthquake and then pulls out the egg to show him. Ah-zaah's eyes open very wide and both of his eyebrows are raised way up as he inspects the egg.

Then he speaks, almost in a whisper, "You kids have got yourselves a dragon egg! The dragons must have hidden it up there on the top of those tent rocks and covered it with mud to disguise it. I told you last week at the campfire that they are expecting the birth of a dragon the night of the July full moon. That's just a few days away."

"But how are the dragons going to find this egg if we have it?" Emily worries.

"What are we going to do?" Clare adds with much concern. "We can't put it back."

Ah-zaah advises, "The best thing you can do is let it hatch and then return the baby dragon to its parents. We will need to find out where to take it. Let's do this. I will go into Bland and talk to Effie Jinks, the owner of the Exchange Hotel. Effie Jinks is a dragon master so she will know where the dragons live."

Then he adds, "I have been watching that Professor and he is acting sneaky. He will be leaving again tomorrow so maybe you kids could check out his cabin. I know he is hiding something. We also need to be careful with that dragon dust you found on the cave floor because it has magical powers."

Just then, Mark pulls out his dagger and it starts to glow…it has dragon dust on it.

Chapter 7
Investigations & Ah-zaah's Trip

In the morning, the Professor and Wong Way pack up their supplies and take the trail towards the Valles Caldera. Mom is a little surprised when Emily offers to change the sheets and sweep up the Professor's cabin. She reminds her not to touch anything. Emily grabs the key to the cabin, the clean sheets, and the broom.

Emily meets Mark and Clare at the Professor's cabin and she carefully opens the door. There are many books on the tables and a bunch of fossils in the corner of the room.

The room is stinky and smells like old farts. Holding her nose Emily says, "We better open the windows and air this place out." With the windows open, it also gives the room more light so they can see better. Clare moves over to the table. She calls to Mark and Emily to come over so she can show them what she has discovered . . . some writing on paper.

"LOOK! This writing looks like the runes we saw on the cave walls. Each mark stands for a different letter of ours." Clare pulls out a pencil and paper from her pocket and writes them down.

She looks up at Mark and Emily and says, "I'm going back to my cabin and study this and I will meet you at the picnic table later to tell you what I find out."

Emily tells Mark, "I better change these sheets while you look around some more."

Mark carefully examines things around the room. Mark wonders aloud. "I see lots of books about fossils and here are some notes on the desk. They are kind of hard to read but here is something else. I think this says '**Draco** Americanus Mex.' Doesn't Draco mean dragon? Isn't one of the constellations in the sky called

Draco? Why would the Professor be interested in dragons?"

After Emily finishes the beds, she and Mark close the windows, lock up the cabin and return the key. Then they go find Clare at the picnic table by the pond.

Clare has compared the writing that she found in the Professor's cabin with the writing she had found in the cave. She looks up when they approach and she tells them, "I have figured it out. It means lair of Thor . . . and I think Thor must be one of the dragons."

Mark then says, "I think there's a marking similar to one of those runes on my dagger too." He pulls out his dagger and they see the symbol "Z" stamped in the metal. Clare replies, "That is definitely a runes letter."

At the same time that Mark, Emily, and Clare are in the cabin, Ah-zaah goes to Bland on his horse. It isn't easy to get there from the Guest Ranch. He travels down Pines Canyon, it turns into Cochiti Canyon, that skirts Cochiti Mesa, and to Young's Apple Orchard before he travels back up Bland Canyon to the town of Bland, now considered a ghost town.

"It means lair of Thor."

38

Ah-zaah knew some history about Bland. He had heard that during the mining boom, there were about 3,000 people in the 60-foot wide Bland Canyon. He also heard that one family even had to put their **outhouse** in the front yard because there wasn't any room in the back of the house. Back then, Bland had two hotels and a newspaper, "The Bland Herald," but today there is only the Exchange Hotel and some other run-down buildings.

He goes to the hotel to visit with Effie Jinks, the owner, and guardian spirit of Bland. She is at the front desk. Effie, a rugged but small woman, is around 50 years old. He asks her if they could talk in private, so they go back to her office and close the door.

Ah-zaah tells Effie about the trip the kids took over to Thor's lair, and what Mark, Emily, and Clare had found.

He says to Effie, "I sent Toco along to keep an eye on them, and because they were so interested in the dragon tales, I asked Toco to show them the old dragon's lair. I figured they would get a kick out of seeing it. I knew Thor had moved up into the Valles Caldera and was no longer in that lair. When the kids returned later that day, they told me what they had found. They had copied the runes from the cave walls and collected some dragon dust from the floor. Emily had even found a blue opal outside the cave. After they started back, they said there was an earthquake and that during the earthquake, when they were passing the tent rocks, a dragon egg, hidden there by the dragons, was dislodged and fell onto the road. They brought it back with them. Later when they wiped off the dirt and **candled** it they could see the dragon inside it."

Ah-zaah reminds Effie, "You and me both know it's getting close to the night of the full moon when the dragons will attempt to retrieve that egg."

He also tells her, "There is a very odd person and his manservant staying at the Guest Ranch. His name is Professor Harold P. Shuttlebutt, and his manservant's name is Wong Way. They use the Ranch as a base camp and go up into the Valles Caldera for a week at a time. . . looking for dinosaur fossils . . . that's what the Professor is telling the Dawson's, but I have a feeling they are looking for that dragon egg; too."

Effie says, "I've also seen a couple of miners who have been hanging around. They seem shifty. They're camped over at the Lone Star Mine. You may want to try to see what they are doing before you head back. I hope you can tell me what you find out about those two dudes. Also, when you come back in the morning, I will draw you a map to where the dragons are and show you the signs to look for to help you find the dragons in the Jemez Mountains."

In the morning, Ah-zaah and Effie exchange information and bid each other farewell. Ah-zaah gets on his horse and heads back to the Guest Ranch.

Chapter 8
Sharing News

It is very dark and late when Ah-zaah returns, so the kids don't get to see him until the next morning after Mark and Emily finish their chores.

Mark and Emily find Clare and they all go over to the barn where Ah-zaah is. They are so excited they can hardly wait to tell him what they discovered about the Puffessor and that they think he may know something about the dragons.

Emily starts, "I told mom I would straighten up the Puffessor's cabin. When I got to the cabin, Mark and Clare were already there.

After we got inside, we saw many books on the table and fossils on the floor. I changed the sheets while Mark and Clare looked around."

Clare says, "I saw some notes on the Puffessor's desk that had runes on them, so I copied them down. Because I figured out how to read runes, I compared those runes to the ones we saw in the cave. They said something about the lair of Thor. We were all thinking Thor was one of the dragons."

Mark tells Ah-zaah, "I was hoping I would find out if the Puffessor knew anything about the dragons, but all I found was some stuff about Draco the dragon constellation. We all wondered why the Puffessor would be interested in that constellation."

Ah-zaah tells the kids their investigating is helpful. Then he tells them about his trip. "I went to see Effie Jinks, the guardian spirit in Bland, who told me about a couple of miners camping up at the Lone Star mine. She suggested I go see what they were up to so I rode up the canyon until I got close to the mine. I could see a tent, a fire circle and the entrance to the mine. I decided to stay out of sight until dark. When it was dark enough, I moved in closer but stayed well hidden. The two men were cooking a pot of beans. As they ate their grub and poured themselves some coffee, the bigger one started talking.

He said, "Well, Bullwhip, soon there will be a full moon, and 'cordin to that information, we need to head on over to the tent rocks to see if the dragons have themselves a new baby dragon. Then we just have to follow 'em up to the Valles Caldera and find their lair. That shouldn't be too hard with this glass gem we got off that dyin' fellow we found over at the Evan-Griffin place."

The other one said, "You're right Curly. That old **codger** told us he was a dragon master and the glass gem had powers. Look, you can see his face burned into it. He said the glass eye gem could be used to find dragons because it lights up when dragons are close by. If we can find that baby dragon, it could lead us to their dragon lair. We just have to figure out how to get the gold and silver out of that lair without gettin' fried. Then we'll be rich dudes."

Ah-zaah continues telling the kids, "When I had heard enough, I slipped away into the dark. The next day I went back to the Exchange Hotel and found Effie and I told her she was right about those two miners and they have a dragon eye gem that they got off some dead guy up at the Evan-Griffin place."

Then Effie got really upset and said, "Old Fred Griffin lived up there. I haven't seen him this year. He was a dragon master, and the miners must have gotten a hold of his dragon eye gem. The dragons used their flame to burn Fred's image into it. I think those two miners are up to no good."

Ah-zaah then reaches into his pocket and pulls out a piece of paper with a map on it that Effie had given him. He continues telling the kids.

Effie also told me, "The dragons carve symbols in the rocks to show how to find other dragons. They use the letters X and Z of the runes alphabet and the dragons turn the letters in different directions pointing the way. After the new baby dragon hatches, you need to sprinkle some magic gold dust on yourself and some on the baby dragon. Then you will be able to talk to each other. The baby dragon will have small wings when it hatches so it won't be able to fly just yet. Don't feed him apples because apples will give him a bellyache. He will bond with the first person he sees and think that person is his mother. He will not be able to breathe fire just yet so you don't need to worry about that, but you do need to be careful because dragon's teeth are very sharp."

Mark says, "Looks like we have a lot of good information. I believe both the Puffessor and the miners are up to no good, and we need to keep our guard up."

Chapter 9
July's Full Moon

That afternoon a couple of grimy looking guys ride into the Guest Ranch. The kids see dad talking to them. Once they leave, the kids run over to see what that was all about. Dad tells them, "They are a couple of miners, looking for an old mine in this area and they have a map. They showed it to me, but it didn't look like anything around here. They are camping by the tent rocks, and said they would be moving on tomorrow."

The kids go over to the barn, where they relay to Ah-zaah what their dad had said. Ah-zaah worries, "I think it's those two miners I saw at Bland."

The kids go back to the picnic table and Mark points out, "I bet they are going to try to pull something, maybe try to steal the baby dragon. They could hold it for ransom to get into the dragon's lair. Let's watch them closely."

Mark has been watching the moon and it's getting fuller. He tells Emily and Clare, "Tonight the moon will be full, and it will peek over the mountains around eight."

That night they meet out in the parking area with Ah-zaah to watch the moonrise. It slowly moves up into the sky. They can see the dragons flying in front of it. They fly around the tent rock area like a swarm of bees, and then they leave.

Effie had told Ah-zaah that the mother dragon would hover over the egg and when it hatches, the baby dragon would slide onto her back.

Clare looks confused and says, "How can she do that?" Ah-zaah tells her, "They were the only dragon species that could hover in the air like a helicopter."

Still wondering, Clare asks, "After the dragon hatches, we will have to figure out how to return it to the parents."

Ah-zaah cautions, "Let's just take one step at a time." The kids head to the coop to wait for the hatching.

The miners are also watching the full moon rise. It is gigantic when it first peeks over the mesa. Curly pulls Fred's glass gem out of his pocket and it starts to glow, so they know the dragons are close. Looking up, the miners see the dragons' **silhouettes** pass in front of the moon. The dragons are circling the tent rocks and making chattering sounds. The miners can tell the dragons are upset and then they see them leave. They decide that the dragons did not find the baby dragon, so Bullwhip suggests to go back to the Guest Ranch in the morning and see what they can find out over there.

Mark, Emily, and Clare enter the chicken coop where earlier they had covered the egg with straw. Removing the straw, they can see that the egg is glowing. The kids place it in the middle of the floor. It is warm to the touch. Sitting in a circle around it, they can hear tapping noises inside it, and then all three of them see a small crack and watch, as it gets bigger. Finally, Mark, Emily, and Clare can see his little horn breaking out of the eggshell.

Suddenly the baby dragon slithers out of the eggshell. He looks up at Emily and she feels an instant connection with him. He is about the size of a large cat, but when he stretches out, he is maybe three feet long. His body is **iridescent** purple with a yellow belly, and his wings are rainbow colors. He flaps them a couple of times. Emily reaches out to him and he slides onto her lap. They are all amazed.

Clare speaks up, "His wings look like a rainbow. Let's call him Bow, for short."

Emily has the dragon dust in a small silk bag in her pocket. She pulls out the dragon dust and sprinkles a little on Bow and themselves.

A magical thing happens. Emily does not open her mouth, she just thinks, "Welcome Bow." Bow looks into her eyes, and asks, "Who are you?"

"I am Emily and this is Clare and that is my brother Mark. We will protect you and take you to your dragon family as soon as we can."

Bow seems to be excited and slithers around the chicken coop. They make a bed of straw for him and settle him down. They promise they will be back in the morning. Emily waits until he is sleeping before she leaves.

Early the next morning Emily hurries into the kitchen and Pilar greets her. Grabbing the egg basket, she tells Pilar she will go collect eggs for breakfast.

When she gets to the chicken coop she slowly opens the door. There are feathers flying everywhere. The chickens are all screeching. There sits Bow in one of the nests eating chicken eggs. He has a large grin on his egg-covered face.

He looks up at her and says, "I was hungry."

Emily didn't realize they needed to feed him. She also thinks they need to find a better place to hide him. He comes over to her and wraps his long body over her shoulders in a loving way.

She tells him, "I have to do a few things and then I will come back with Mark and Clare." She collects the rest of the eggs but leaves a few for Bow and puts the chickens in the outside pen.

Back in the kitchen, Emily tells Pilar, "It looks like something got into the chicken coop last night and we lost a few eggs."

"I was hungry."

Pilar explains, "That's OK. We don't need as many eggs because the Benson's moved out of the Blue Bell cabin yesterday and it will be empty for a week or so. Please have Mark patch up any holes he finds in the chicken coop."

Outside, Emily looks around and sees Mark. She tells him what happened in the chicken coop.

Mark suggests, "What about putting Bow in the Blue Bell cabin and then we'll find him some food."

Emily continues, "Would Pepper mind if we gave Bow some of her table scraps? We could also see if he will eat dog food."

"That's a great idea." Mark smiles and asks, "Can I have some of that dragon dust?"

Emily hands him the small pouch of magic dust. He goes over to Pepper and sprinkles some on her.

Pepper responds, "Bark! Bark! Go for a walk? Go for a walk?" Mark asks her about the table scraps and dog food, and Pepper answers back, "Bark! Bark! Well if I have to, well if I have to." Pepper barks again, "There are **varmints** around the cabins. Maybe he would like those? But, don't let him under the Professor's cabin. There's a skunk that lives under it."

"Oh . . . that's why it smells so bad in there," Mark laughs.

That morning, the miners slip into the Guest Ranch unnoticed. Curly is holding the glass eye gem. As they sneak around the cabins, the gem starts to glow. They watch the kids go into the Blue Bell cabin carrying something wrapped in a blanket. "Look," Bullwhip says in a soft voice, "I bet they have that dragon. You know if we can get the baby dragon, we can use it for ransom for the dragon's gold. Let's hang around here and see what those kids are up to."

Chapter 10
4th of July Excitement

The clouds are starting to build up in the afternoons. July brings the **monsoons** so it rains almost every afternoon, sometimes a little and other times a lot. If it rains a lot, the streams will overflow their banks.

It is time to figure out when and how to get Bow home. The kids meet at the Blue Bell cabin. Bow is waiting for them. Mark brings Bow some table scraps. In just two days, they can see Bow is already getting bigger. They let him out to play in the tall grass behind the cabin.

Mark informs the girls, "I have a plan. First, we need to approach mom and dad about going on a camping trip up into the Valle Grande."[12]

A few summers ago, Mark had camped all over the Jemez Mountains with the **Boy Scouts**. He was able to attend the Los Alamos Ranch School[13] summer program through a scholarship the Ranch School had set up. The school had been running since 1917 and is located on a mesa on the east side of the Jemez Mountain Range.

Last summer, the kids had also camped at Graduation Flats a few times.

Mark explains to Emily and Clare, "I don't see why our parents wouldn't let us go into the Valle Grande; I'm 16, an Eagle Scout, and as long as we take Toco with us, he can fly back every day and check in at the Guest Ranch. Toco can tell Ah-zaah who can tell our parents where we are."

Mark pulls out a **topo** map that has drawings of the mountains, valleys, lakes, rivers, and forests, along with roads and trails of the area. Then he opens the map Effie had drawn of the area and spreads them both out on the table to compare them.

Mark studies the maps and tells them, "We will need to take the Bland Frijoles trail southwest, and then travel across Cochiti Mesa and drop down into Canon del Norte. There is water there and a road in the bottom that will take us right up into the Valle Grande, the south end of the Valles Caldera."

Emily studies Effie's hand-drawn map and compares it to the topo map. She points out, "It looks like the dragons are in the Valle Toledo area. That's on the far side of the Valles Caldera."

Mark continues, "The Boy Scouts have a camp at Rio de los Indios, but they don't like to go into the Valle Toledo because there are a lot of deer flies there. They have a vicious bite."

Clare adds, "We better take some **bug juice** repellent with us."

Clare looks at the map legend and they see a question in her eyes as she is trying to figure something out.

She informs Mark and Emily, "It looks like it's about 16 miles to get to the edge of the Caldera, and a horse travels about 4 miles an hour. Therefore, it would take us 4, no, let's say 5 hours, counting going up and down the mesas and canyons to reach that point."

Emily comments, "There is the old Nugget Mine in the bottom of Canon del Norte, too. Let's make sure we bring flashlights to check it out. We can also stop at the **Santuario** a little further up the canyon."

"That reminds me, we need a list of all the things we have to take," adds Clare.

She pulls out a piece of paper and writes down things like flashlights, bug juice, bedrolls, and food.

Emily speaks up, "It may take us a few days to locate the dragons' home and find Bow's parents and another day back. Let's tell mom and dad we will be gone 5 days."

Now it's time to bring the camping trip idea to their parents. Clare goes and gets her mom and dad and they all meet at the main house with Mark and Emily's parents. They present their ideas, and because they have a solid plan, their parents tell them they can go. The kids decide they will leave the next day since they will be having a 4th of July celebration at the campfire that night.

The miners also have been making plans. They had been watching the kids for a few days and they know the dragon is in the last cabin. They decide they should sneak into the ranch when everyone is at the campfire celebrating the 4th of July and steal him.

That night, Ah-zaah builds a large campfire. The Professor and Wong Way, who are in the camp now, decide to join them. They all sit around the campfire singing patriotic songs. It gets dark, and Wong Way brings out a bunch of fireworks. He lights them, and the fireworks show is amazing.

He then looks down at the remaining fireworks and says, "I'm sure I brought more. I must have dropped some on the way over here."

Just then, another large fireworks display goes off, but this one is over by the Blue Bell cabin. The kids jump up and run over to the cabin hoping Bow is OK. Reaching the cabin, they see the door is open. Bow is sitting on the ground in front of the cabin.

"What happened?" They say together.

"The fire from my mouth lit the fireworks."

Bow cries, "I was in my bed and two guys broke open the door. They saw me but I was able to slip outside. They were trying to catch me when I saw those fireworks on the ground. I was so scared that when I opened my mouth, fire exploded from it. The fire from my mouth lit the fireworks and they blew up in their faces. They both took off running down the road."

The kids get Bow settled back in the cabin and realize they need to guard him more closely. Mark offers to stay with him in the cabin that night.

Chapter 11
Capture & Rescue

Mark, Emily, and Clare got their supplies together the day before, so all they need to do this morning is saddle up the horses and pack the mule.

Mark shows them how to make sure the load on the mule is the same weight on both sides. He teaches the girls how to tie a diamond knot that he had learned at the Los Alamos Ranch School summer camp. The diamond knot is very strong but also forms a decorative loop in the shape of a diamond. After they tie up their load, they slip Bow into one of Emily's saddlebags and open the top a little so he can look out. They figure he will sleep most of the day since dragons are mostly **nocturnal**.

They pass the tent rocks and look for signs of the miners. They are hoping never to see them again. Soon they are in Pines, where the trailhead starts. The trail is steep as the kids guide the horses up to the mesa top. They stay on top for a few miles then drop sharply into Paso Del Norte Canyon. They reach the road in the bottom where a small stream is running alongside it. The horses drink from the stream. The girls see a cabin further up the road. Mark shouts to them, "There's the Nugget Mine."

The entrance opens in the wall of a large cliff. An ore car track disappears into the mouth of the opening and an old ore car sits at the end of the track. Next to the opening are parts of a **sluice box** lying on the ground. The sluice box was once used to divert the water from the nearby stream.

Clare suggests they stop for lunch and explore a little. They hobble the horses and eat more of Pilar's great food. It starts to sprinkle, so they decide to get out of the rain for a while.

Mark says, "Let's check out the mine. He grabs the flashlight and leads the way.

Bow wraps himself around Emily's shoulders but once they get inside the mine, he suddenly wants down.

Bow gets all excited, "I smell gold in here." Emily lets him down, and he slithers around the rocks.

Next, they hear him say, "I found some!"

They go over to where he is. He opens his mouth. Flames come out and he melts the gold out of the rocks.

"Don't touch it," cautions Clare, "Wait until it cools down."

After the gold has cooled, Mark picks it up and says, "I will carry it for you Bow," and places it in his pocket.

They head back to the front opening of the mine. The rain has stopped. Their eyes are adjusting to the light, but before they know what is happening, the barrel of a gun is pointing right in their faces.

"Move over there," Bullwhip demands.

Curly is holding a birdcage and he orders Emily, "Put that slimy rainbow thing in this birdcage."

She picks up Bow and puts him in the cage.

Then he insists, "Put this lock on the door," and he hands her the lock.

Bullwhip now orders, "Move over by that sluice box."

Curly puts the cage with Bow in it on a lantern pole hook next to the cave opening. He motions the kids to sit down next to the sluice box and he ties them securely to it.

Curly mutters, "That oughtta hold 'em. Let's take this scummy thing over to the cabin."

They move the cage to another hook over at the cabin about fifty feet away so the kids can't hear what they are saying.

Just then, they see Toco circling in the sky. He comes down and lands next to Mark. Mark tells Toco to go behind them and untie the knots. Toco gets behind the sluice box and has them untied in no time.

Just then, they see something move over in the meadow. Clare's eyes get really big and she speaks very softly, "It's a bear."

It's moving closer to them so Mark says quickly, "I have an idea. Emily, get out the dragon dust and hold up a pinch of it for Toco."

Mark directs Toco to fly over to the bear and sprinkle some dust on his head.

As requested, Toco flies up and circles the bear. The bear sees him; he stands up and swats at him but Toco is too fast and sprinkles the dust on the bear's head. The kids hear both of them talking.

The bear promises, "I was just funning you. I wouldn't hurt you."

"I know that," assures Toco, and then he adds, "You're really just a great big teddy bear at heart."

As the bear comes closer to them, he makes a grunting sound and says, "You guys look like you could use some help."

"We sure can," exclaims Clare. "Those two guys at that cabin tied us up and took our friend."

Mark then adds, "I have an idea. Why don't you just quietly walk over behind them and when you get real close, stand up and roar."

"Will do," says the bear.

They watch as the bear moves silently through the tall grass. When he is just inches behind the miners, he stands up and with a bellow heard all the way across the meadow, gives out his biggest roar. The men take one look at the bear, jump up and take off running up the road with the bear chasing right after them. It didn't take long before the bear had them treed.

Clare goes over to the miner's horses, unties them and shoos them down the canyon. Mark and Emily go to the cabin. Mark pulls out his dagger and uses the point to unlock the cage. He opens it and Bow jumps into Emily's arms.

Clare reaches the cabin and looks down where the miners had been standing. She can see something glowing on the ground. It looks like a round glass rock. Clare picks up the glass rock and realizes that it's the dragon eye gem with Fred Griffin's face burned into it. She puts it in her pocket. They collect the miner's guns and hide them.

Bow jumps into Emily's arms.

"Let's get out of here," Mark orders. They climb on their horses, put Bow back in Emily's saddlebag and start up the road past the miners where the bear is dancing around the tree. The bear yells, "How long do you want me to keep them up there?" Mark answers. "Maybe 20 minutes because the miners still have to get to their horses that are way down the road."

Then Pepper barks, "Thanks bear. Thanks bear."

Heading up the canyon, the kids stop at the Santuario where there is a statue of the Blessed Virgin Mary. Next to the statue, they find candles. They light a candle and pray for a safe trip. Mounting their horses, they head up the canyon until it ends and the road divides.

Mark points to the right saying, "That road goes over to Graduation Flats, but let's take the left road. It will take us to the edge of the Valle Grande,[12] which is located on the south side of the Valles Caldera. We can make camp over there next to the Jemez River."

"Oh look!" Clare spots, "There is one of those runes carved into the rock. It is pointing the direction we need to go. It will lead us down into the Valle Grande."

The road curves around the side of the mountain and soon they are looking down into the vast valley. "What is that? Snow?" wonders Clare aloud.

"No," Mark replies. "Those are sheep. I've heard there are as many as 30,000 down there. We best head toward the East Fork of the Jemez River down that way and to the left."

They make camp next to the stream, build a fire and cook some food. Before they know it, night comes and they crawl into their bedrolls. The moon is still big but no longer full. Mark points out the **Big Dipper and Little Dipper.**

He tells the girls, "Now follow the two stars at the front of the Big Dipper and you will come to the North Star which is the end of the handle of the Little Dipper. Now, this part is a little harder. The stars that curve around the Little Dipper point to a square that is the Draco constellation."

"I see it now," says Clare.

Their conversation went on for a few more minutes, and then they all fell asleep.

Chapter 12
Dragons in the Hot Springs

As the sun peeks over the mountains, Mark, Emily, and Clare decide to head northeast towards the flock of sheep. They come to a couple of herders who greet them, "Hola." Mark and Emily reply, "Hola," and Mark starts talking to them in Spanish.

He asks them, "Have you seen any new people in this area?"

The older of the two replies, "Yes, the Boy Scouts came through a few days ago. It looks like they were headed up north."

"Yes," Mark tells them. "They have a camp up there in that area."

"Oh," says the second guy. "We also saw a couple of odd ones this morning. A big guy who had a Chinese man with him. They headed north, also."

Emily adds, "That sounds like the Puffessor and Wong Way."

They leave the herders and Clare remarks, "Gee, I didn't know you two spoke Spanish."

Mark tells Clare, "Yes, our mother is Spanish. She told us our ancestors came from Spain, and they settled in the Rio Grande Valley in 1674. They were one of the founding families of New Mexico. She taught us Spanish when we were little."

Then they tell Clare what the sheepherders had said.

"Well, let's get moving," Mark, advises. Then he calls Pepper.

She comes running up to him. He says to her, "Where have you been?"

Bark! Bark! "I was just talking to that sheepdog over there. He had a lot to tell me. He knows about the dragons. He has seen them flying around at night."

72

"Does he know where they live?" Emily asked.

Pepper barks and answers, "He says they are all over. You just have to look for their signs. He said he could smell them all over the place. He did suggest we might check out the hot springs over by San Antonio Creek[14] on the west side of the Valles Caldera. He thought we might find some of them in the hot springs there."

"Let's head that way," declares Clare.

They mount up and start up the trail next to the San Antonio Creek. The clouds are starting to build up, but the rain has held off. After a few miles, the trail turns east, then north, then east again. Finally, they come to the headwaters of San Antonio Creek. They are getting closer to the springs.

Mark suggests, "We better be quiet until we get to the springs."

Sure enough, they hear noises as they approach; sitting in the springs are two dragons.

Clare suggests, "Let's send Bow in to make contact with them."

Bow pokes his head out of the saddlebag and then jumps to the ground. He slips through the grass and up to the spring. The kids can all hear the dragons talking.

Bow, with a nervous voice, says, "Hi. My name is Bow and my friends are trying to help me find my parents. They were wondering if you could help us."

One of the dragons exclaims, "My, my! You are the missing baby dragon! Your parents had put your egg on top of those tent rocks and covered the shell with mud so it looked like a rock. They were so upset when they went to get you and you weren't there. My name is Askook and this is Chua. Ask your friends to join us and we will see if we can help."

Emily, Mark, and Clare go up the hill to join Bow by the pool. There in front of them are two full-grown dragons. Emily's eyes are as big as saucers as she stares at them.

Emily bows to them and then finds her voice, "Hi. I'm Emily and that's Mark and Clare."

She explains how they had found Bow's egg on the road next to the tent rocks, and that after the earthquake, they had taken the egg home, watched Bow hatch, and now they are trying to take him to his parents.

"My, my! You are the missing baby dragon."

Chua addresses them and because of dragon magic, they all understand each other, "Bow, your parents are Fagon and Chusi and their lair is in the Valle Toledo area."

Mark offers, "I think that's close to where the Boy Scouts are camping."

Askook suggests, "We could take Bow back with us but his wings aren't strong enough to fly that far."

"Bow," Chua adds, "We can fly over to your parents this evening and let them know you are coming."

"That's a great idea," exclaims Clare. "We'll just camp here and hang out with you this afternoon."

They set up camp, put on their swimming suits, and jump into the hot springs.

That evening they build a fire. When it gets dark, Chua speaks up. "Let's play guess who? It's a riddle game. I'll start. What is always coming but never arrives?"

"That's a hard one," says Clare.

"Let me tell you," laughs Chua. "It's tomorrow. Now you give us one, Clare."

"OK, why do dragons sleep all day?" asks Clare.

"Why?" wonders Emily.

Clare responds, "The dragons were avoiding the knights all night." The kids laugh.

Askook and Chua look at each other with questioning looks. Chua says, "We don't get it."

Mark explains, "In a land called Europe, men dressed up in metal armor. They were called knights, and they went out to hunt dragons . . . at night."

It finally gets dark enough for Askook and Chua to leave. The kids wish them a safe trip. Mark tells them not to worry . . . there are no knights around here. Emily promises Askook and Chua they will see them the next day. Askook says he and Chua will tell Bow's parents he is coming to them tomorrow.

Chapter 13
Bow is Captured Again

The next day they are up early to get a good start. Going back over their tracks east for a few miles, they come to a fork in the trail. They see a rock with a runes carving that points northeast. Clare pulls out the Fred Griffin glass eye gem but it isn't glowing. The trail crosses the San Luis Creek. They come to a more heavily used trail going farther south and another carving on a rock. They don't go far on this trail before they notice some fresh mounds of dirt off the side of the trail.

"Let's check it out," suggests Mark as they get down from the horses. Emily puts Bow on her shoulders and they head over to the digging area.

Emily thinks aloud, "I wonder if this is where the Puffessor is digging."

They see a place that looks like it could be a campsite. As they are inspecting it, all at once they hear a loud sound over their heads. The next thing they know a huge heavy net covers all of them. From behind some bushes, appear the Professor and Wong Way.

The Professor is jumping up and down yelling, "We got him! We got him! I am going to be famous! Wong Way, go get that crate off the pack mule and put that dragon in it."

Wong Way follows the Professor's orders. He takes the crate over to where Bow is stuck under the net. He opens the crate, cuts a small hole in the net and forces Bow into the crate.

Professor shouts, "Let's get out of here!"

"What about children?" yells Wong Way.

"We will be long gone before they get out from under that net," answers the Professor.

They load the crate with Bow in it onto the pack mule and head down the trail. Clare tries to move under the net but it is too heavy. "Hold on," Mark says as he reaches around his belt and finds his dagger. With a few strokes, he frees himself. He then goes over and frees the girls and Pepper.

"We sure didn't see that coming," gasps Emily. "How are we going to get Bow back?"

Mark thinks for a moment and suggests, "Let's get back to the horses and ride until we get to an open area where we can see them ahead on the trail."

They mount their horses and gallop down the trail. The valley opens up, and they can see the Professor and Wong Way off in the distance. Mark pulls out his binoculars. He can see them about a mile ahead. As he scans the whole area, he can also see the Boy Scouts fishing in Jaramillo Creek. Also, over on a side road, he sees a man on horseback, who has a dog with him. The kids get off their horses and lay the map out on the ground.

"We are here," Mark, points out. "The Scouts are fishing over there. The man on the horse is here."

Emily asks, "Do you think the Puffessor and Wong Way are going back to the Guest Ranch? We could just go back there."

Clare tells the others, "I think they might be headed somewhere else because the sooner they get that dragon to civilization, the sooner the Puffessor will become famous. You heard him. We need to figure out how to get Bow back as quickly as possible."

Mark studies the map and says, "It looks like there are two ways the Puffessor and Wong Way could go. One is west. . . that would take them through Jemez Springs and to Albuquerque, or they could head east to the Los Alamos Ranch School, then head down the mesa and catch the Chili Line[15] railroad at Otowi Bridge."

Just then, Toco shows up. Mark asks, "Where have you been?"

He quorks, "Well I reported home and then I decided to look for the dragon's lair, and I found it. I also found the Boy Scouts camped over in the Valle de los Poso and saw our friend the brown bear near the fork in the road. Finally, I saw a man with his dog. He is riding his horse on the road over by Rabbit Mountain."

Clare adds, "Well we really don't know which way the Puffessor is going until he gets over there."

She points to a spot on the map where one road meets the other.

Mark informs them, "I have a plan. Toco, you fly back and ask the bear to go to that spot on the map and stop the Puffessor from going any farther. Emily, you and Clare take Pepper and talk to the man on the horse. Ask for his help. I will go and ask the Boy Scouts to help us. We will all meet at that spot on the map where the trail meets the road."

Chapter 14
Boy Scouts Help

Mark gallops down the trail and reaches the Boy Scouts.

He sees his old **patrol** leader and calls out. "Hi Tom, I need some help!"

Mark jumps off his horse, the other Boy Scouts crowd around him. "How can we help?" asks Tom.

"Have you seen that old fuddy-duddy guy hanging around here with his Chinese man-servant?"

They shake their heads and one of the Scouts speaks up and says, "No, we haven't seen them."

Mark then tells Tom and the Scouts, "Well this morning that guy trapped me, my sister, and our friend under a net and stole something that belongs to us. We were able to get loose and send Toco, our raven, and our friend the brown bear to stop them at the intersection in the road. They won't be able to hold them for much longer. Do you think you could help us?"

The boys all nod their heads yes. "For sure. What can we do?" Tom offers.

"One more thing I need to tell you," declares Mark, "You will all have to take an oath of secrecy."

"Golly," says one of the Scouts. "Why so secret? What's the big deal?"

"You will understand when you agree," replies Mark.

They all agree. They raise their right hand and Mark says, "**Boy Scout Troop #22** promises to keep secret forever what I am about to tell you."

After they all agree, one of the boys asks, "So what's the big secret?"

Mark replies, "The item they stole is a baby dragon we are trying to return to his parents."

"A dragon?" One Scout exclaims.

"No fooling?" another boy adds.

Tom commands the patrol, "Let's get going. No time to waste."

Then Tom sends two of the Scouts back to the camp with the fish they had caught. He instructs them to tell the rest of the troop where they are going.

Emily and Clare catch up to the man on the horse. The two dogs run up and greet each other. The man on the horse is slender with a sparkle in his bright blue eyes.

Emily starts the conversation "Hi, I'm Emily and this is my friend Clare and that's Pepper," pointing to the dog.

Clare jumps in, "We have a big problem. We are from the Tent Rock Guest Ranch and are camping in the Valles Caldera. This morning a crazy man trapped us under a large heavy net and took our friend Bow who we have been trying to take to his parents.

Emily speaks up, "My brother Mark has gone to get help from the Boy Scouts and we are all meeting over where the trail intersects with the road to stop that crazy man. Do you think you could help us?"

"Well," he answers, "My name is Robert Oppenheimer[16] and I have a place over by Cowles. I am just checking out this area."

He seems trustworthy thought Emily so she asks him, "Can you keep a secret?"

"Not a problem. It won't be the first one or the last one I will ever have to keep," he replies with a smile.

Emily speaks softly like the world could hear. "Our friend Bow is a dragon, and the Professor is a paleontologist who is going to exploit him to the world so that he can become rich and famous."

"Well then let's get going," he offers. "By the way, my friends call me Oppie."

Meanwhile, Mark and the Boy Scouts can see a bunch of birds flying in circles over at the intersection. As the boys get closer they can tell the birds are dropping pinecones on something below and can hear the bear roaring. The

Professor and Wong Way are prancing around trying to dodge the pinecones. Mark calls out to Toco and the bear, telling them to back off. The Scouts surround the dragon snatchers on their horses.

Mark dismounts and demands, "Professor, you have something that belongs to us."

"No I don't," he protests.

Mark requests, "Tom, will you and Patrick go over to the pack mule and get that crate?"

Just then, Emily and Clare show up with Oppie. Emily opens the crate and out slides Bow. He looks rattled but Emily picks him up.

Bow is in tears and speaks softly, "You guys saved me."

Mark then realizes that others can't understand him. He asks Emily for the dragon dust and tells Toco to put a pinch on everyone. Then everyone can understand what's being said. Oppie offers to take the Professor and Wong Way down to Fuller Lodge in Los Alamos and get the **headmaster**, to put them on the train to Santa Fe.

Tom suggests, "Oppie, these two may be a handful. Let me send a few of my older Scouts to accompany you."

Professor balks, "What about my belongings at the Guest Ranch?"

Mark responds, "I will let my parents know you aren't coming back and have them box up your stuff and take it down to the Merc. You can pick it up there. Oh, and by the way, I am telling the dragons to watch out for you and if they ever see you in this area again to make crispy critters out of you."

Oppie and half of the Scout patrol take the Professor and Wong Way east to the Los Alamos Ranch School, and everyone else goes back to the Boy Scout camp, except the bear. Mark thanks the bear for his help, and the bear lumbers back down the road that leads into the valley.

Chapter 15
Sworn to Secrecy

Mark, Emily, Clare, Tom and the rest of the patrol ride into camp and the other Scouts greet them. There are 24 Scouts altogether. They have tents, a campfire circle, and a cooking area. An older man is making supper over a raised **cooking altar**. After they take care of the horses, everyone gathers by the fire circle.

Tom brings the meeting to order and starts to speak. "As some of you know we have been out helping one of our fellow Scouts, Mark, his sister, Emily and their friend, Clare. Mark would like to tell you what is going on."

Mark says, "First, I need to ask everyone if you will be sworn to secrecy." Then he turns to the man cooking and calls out, "That includes you Bences."[17]

They all agree and each person raises his right hand and repeats after saying his own name. "I_____ of Boy Scout Troop #22, promise to keep Mark's secret for the rest of my life."

When they are finished, Emily holds the saddlebag open and out of the top slides Bow onto Emily's shoulders.

"That's unbelievable," gasps one of the boys, as they all stare in surprise. "Even if I did tell people about this they wouldn't believe me."

It wasn't much later, Bences announces supper, and everyone gathers around for the best trout in the world, along with homemade **sopaipillas**.

The Scouts decide to accompany Mark, Emily, Clare, and Bow to the Valle Toledo to find Bow's parents. As the evening comes on, they all sit around the campfire singing.

One of the boys looks over at Clare and tells her, "You left your flashlight on in your pocket."

Clare looks down and sees the dragon eye gem glowing. She forgot she had put it there when Bow had been taken earlier that day. She pulls it out of her shirt pocket and looks at it, as it gets brighter.

She announces, "We are about to have visitors."

They look up and watch as two dragons descend from the night sky.

Mark stands up and greets them, "Hi, Askook and Chua."

Chua says, "We thought you guys were going to make it to the dragon lair today. We have been waiting there for you."

Clare begins, "It seems we found ourselves in a heap of trouble. This man we knew trapped Mark, Emily, Bow and me under a large net. He then crated up Bow, took him down the road, and just left us there under the net. Luckily we were able to free ourselves, and with the help of these Scouts, we were able to get Bow back."

Then Tom adds, "Would you like to join our fire circle?"

Before they know it, Askook and Chua have joined the campfire circle and are telling riddles. Everyone is having a great evening.

Then Askook and Chua inform everyone, "It's time to go. We will see you all tomorrow."

After the dragons take off, a Scout, holding a bugle, moves away from the fire circle. Mark, Clare, and Emily with Bow on her shoulders and all the Scouts stand in a large circle, and the bugle sounds as they all sing **Taps**.

"Day is done, gone the sun,

From the lake, from the hills,

From the sky;

All is well, safely rest, God is nigh."

Chapter 16
Dragon Reunion & Magic

The next morning everyone mounts up and heads to the Valle Toledo. They are all sprinkled with dragon dust and covered with bug juice. Emily leads the group with Bow riding on her shoulders. Mark and Clare follow behind her, and the Scouts form a double line behind them. They are an impressive looking parade. The Scouts wear their Stetson hats and uniforms. After they have been riding several miles, they start to see signs of dragons . . . large piles of blue **scat**. The dragon eye gem in Clare's pocket begins to glow.

The trail opens into a large meadow. One of the Scouts blows his horn announcing their presence. Soon, dragons start appearing and line both sides of the trail greeting everyone. In front of them is the biggest dragon of them all. Emily thinks, "This must be the guardian dragon. He towers over all the others." To the right of him, she thinks might be Bow's parents. Once they reach the dragons, Bow flies off Emily's shoulders and lands in the wings of his mother.

The guardian dragon speaks, "Welcome. My name is **Mexacoatl**. I can't thank you enough for bringing our young one home. Please accept our hospitality."

The Scouts and the kids dismount and they put the horses out to graze. Mexacoatl introduces the kids to Bow's parents, Facon and Chusi. Bow is busy filling in his parents about all the things that had happened.

Mark, Emily, and Clare notice that the Scouts are over by a bunch of young looking dragons and the next thing they know the Scouts are on the dragon's backs flying around in the sky. Mexacoatl asks the kids if they would like to see his lair. The three follow him into a large cave. It is bright inside from all the gold, silver, and other treasures. Clare and Emily try on some of the jewelry and Mark even finds a crown.

Mark shows Mexacoatl his dagger and Mexacoatl states, "It looks like that dagger came from Peru. It can be used to summon an army of dragons."

They go back outside. Clare pulls out Fred Griffin's dragon eye gem. She tells Mexacoatl that Fred Griffin is gone and they want to return the dragon eye gem. Mexacoatl asks Emily to go back in the cave, find three similar glass gems, and bring them to him. She does as he requests. She lays them in front of him on the ground. Mark and Clare stand next to her. Mexacoatl asks them to close their eyes. They all stand with their eyes closed and feel a warm breeze blow over their faces. Mexacoatl then asks them to open their eyes. They look down at the glass gems on the ground. Now they can see their own faces burned into the glass gems.

Mexacoatl explains, "You are now all dragon masters . . . pick up your dragon eye gems." Then Mexacoatl adds, "Clare, I notice you have trouble walking."

She answers, "Yes, I had polio."

Mexacoatl tells her, "Step close to me, my princess." She moves closer, standing within inches of him. She sees the bottom half of his body curled up like a cobra snake. He opens up his wings and wraps them very carefully around her. As Mark and Emily watch, a glow comes out of the top of his wings, he opens them up and Clare steps back.

"Thank you," she whispers to him. She reaches down and takes off her braces. Mark and Emily watch in wonderment as she walks around. She is no longer crippled!

All too soon, it is time for them to leave. They say their goodbyes. Bow promises he will check in on them during the next full moon.

Mexacoatl asks them to come back next summer for Bow's first birthday. He adds, "There will be a big celebration and dragons will come from as far away as Mexico. It will be held at Graduation Flats."

Mark says, "I know where that is. It's not far from the Guest Ranch. It's where we camped last summer."

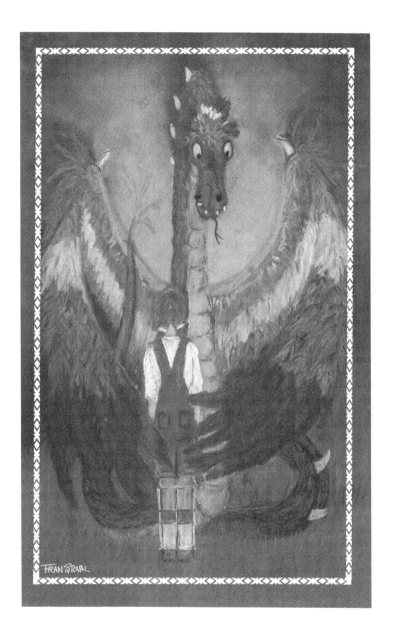

A glow comes out of the top of his wings.

The kids ride out of the meadow. The Boy Scouts ride with them until they come to the edge of their camp. Mark, Emily, and Clare thank them again for all their help. They ride for another hour hoping to get closer to home and end up back on the edge of the Jemez River where they had started. They get out their bedrolls, crawl in, and as they gaze into the darkening sky, they see the dragons flying above them. Waving up at them, Emily thinks, "what a sight," as the dragons circle above.

Chapter 17
Magical Summer

About noon the next day, Mark, Emily, and Clare arrive back at the Guest Ranch.

Their mom sees them first and calls out, "They're back! They're back!" Everyone runs out to greet them. They knew they were coming because Toco had flown ahead to tell Ah-zaah who had told their parents.

When Clare's parents join them, she runs into their arms. They both stare at her legs without braces, and ask, "What happened? Where are your braces?" Clare just grins. The kids had already figured out what they were going to tell everyone.

Clare laughs, "It was at the hot springs. I sat in the water for a couple of hours, and somehow it fixed my legs!"

That evening around the supper table, everyone wants to hear about their trip.

Emily and Mark's mom inquires, "Well, what did you all do?"

Mark starts, "The first day we checked out the Nugget Mine over in Paso Del Norte Canyon and I found some gold." He reaches in his pocket and pulls out the gold that Bow had found in the mine.

Next, Emily tells them, "We stopped at the shrine and saw the Blessed Virgin Mary statue. We lit a candle and prayed for a safe trip. Then we camped on the edge of the Valles Caldera and did some stargazing. Mark showed us how to find the Big Dipper, the Little Dipper, and the constellation Draco."

Mark adds, "Then we stopped and talked to a couple of sheepherders who were taking care of thousands of sheep. After that, we went to the San Antonio Hot Springs, soaked and hung out. Later, we found Boy Scout Troop #22 camping out. They were fishing and they invited us to a fish fry with them."

Clare adds, "Then we met a man named Oppie who said he lives over in Cowles. We also saw the Professor and Wong Way. They told us they were going down to the Los Alamos Ranch School and then to Otowi to catch the train. Oh! They also wanted me to tell you, they are not coming back and have asked that we pack up their things, put them in their car, and drive the car to the Merc so they can pick everything up there."

"I think that's most of it," says Emily. Mark and Clare nod and they all have slight grins on their faces. The three of them look at each other, knowing they were sharing the same thought . . . what a magical summer!

The End

GLOSSARY

Amphitheres – Winged snakes or dragons found in north and south America.

Apache Indian – A member of the Native American Apache tribe in the Southwestern United States.

Appaloosa – An American horse breed best known for its colorful spotted coat pattern.

Arbor – A shelter of vines or branches that are shaped like an arch that plants grow over.

Artifacts – A simple object; a tool or weapon that was made by people long ago.

Bandelier National Monument – A protected area. One of five US National Monuments in the state of New Mexico near Los Alamos.

Big and Little Dipper – Two constellations in the sky. Also known as Ursa Major, (Latin) for Big Bear and Ursa Minor, Little Bear.

Boy Scout – A member of the Boy Scouts of America organization. Encouraging boys to take part in activities outside and become responsible and independent.

Boy Scout Troop #22 – A Boy Scout troop started at the Los Alamos Ranch School in 1918. It is still operating today. (Los Alamos, The Ranch School Years)

Buffalo – A symbolic animal of the Great Plains also known as bison. They are formidable beasts and the heaviest land animals in North America. (National Geographic)

Bug Juice – *Slang* – Insect repellant and later became a brand name.

Caldera – A volcanic feature formed by the collapse of the land surface after a gigantic volcanic eruption. The word *caldera* comes from the Portuguese language, meaning "cauldron." (Kidpeda)

Candled – Holding an egg up to candlelight to see through the shell.

Carrot Top – *Slang* – A person with red hair; a redhead.

Codger – An old man, especially one who is strange or humorous in some way. (Cambridge Dictionary)

Cooking Altar – A raised fire pit built with logs and filled with dirt.

Dagger – A sharp pointed knife for stabbing.

Draco – A constellation in the far northern sky. Its name is Latin for dragon. (Wikipedia)

Fossils – Something like a leaf, skeleton, or foot print that once was a plant or animal in ancient times and is now a rock.

Headmaster – A male teacher in charge of a private school.

Heritage – The background from which one comes from.

Hobble – A short strap tied between the legs of a horse allowing it to wander short distances but preventing it from running off.

Horse Sense – Common sense. Sound and practical judgment.

Indians – The original peoples of the Americas. They were called "Indian" by Christopher Columbus who thought he had arrived in India. Today we respectfully call them Native American.

Iridescent – A lustrous rainbow-like play of color caused by differential refraction of light waves, seen on, rocks, oil slicks, soap bubbles, or fish scales.

Iron Horse – A steam Locomotive.

Knapsack – A bag with shoulder straps carried on the back.

Lair – A dragon's nest and place they keep their treasures.

Mexacoatl – The younger brother of the ancient Aztecs dragon Quetzalcoatl.

Moccasins – A flat shoe made of deerskin or other soft leather, worn by Native Americans.

Monsoons – The rain that falls during the summer season and may cause flooding.

Nocturnal – A term is given to an animal that sleeps mostly in the day and hunts for food during the night.

Nomadic – A group of people who move from place to place instead of living in one place at a time.

Obsidian Rocks – A dark natural glass formed by the rapid cooling of melting lava. (Merriam-Webster.com)

Orchard – A planting of fruit trees, nut trees, or sugar maples. (Merriam-Webster.com)

Opal – A white or clear stone that reflects colors and is used in jewelry.

Outhouse – An outbuilding containing a toilet, with no plumbing.

Pack Mule – The offspring of a donkey and a horse. Used as a beast of burden.

Patrol – A small group of Boy Scouts. Usually around eight boys.

Paleontologist – A scientist who studies fossils.

Petroglyphs – A carving on rocks, made by a member of a prehistoric people.

Plaza – An open public space area, such as a city square.

Polio – A serious disease that affects the nerves of the spine and often makes a person permanently unable to move particular muscles. (Leaner's Dictionary)

Procession – The act of moving along or proceeding in orderly succession, as a line of people, animals, vehicles, etc. (Dictionary.com)

Pueblo Indian – Native Americans in the Southwestern United States who share common agricultural, material and religious practices. (Wikipedia)

Pumice – A porous spongy rock formed of volcanic glass, used as an abrasive.

Roadster – An early automobile having an open body, a single seat for two or three people, and a large trunk or a rumble seat.

Retrace – To go back over.

Rumble Seat – A seat recessed into the back of a coupe or roadster, covered by a hinged lid that opens to form the back of the seat when in use. (Dictionary.com)

Runes – Any of the characters in the alphabets that were used in ancient times by people of Northern Europe. (Leaner's Dictionary)

Santuario – Spanish for Sanctuary, a place to worship.

Scat – Animal feces, poop.

Shaman – A person who is believed in some cultures to be able to use magic to cure people who are sick, to control future events.

Silhouette – The outline or general shape of something. A dark image outlined against a lighter background. (Dictionary.com)

Sluice Box – A long, narrow box that water passes through when putting it into a creek or stream. Used to separate the ore from the rock. (Wikipedia)

Squash Blossom Necklace – Designed to resemble the flower of the squash plant.

Sopaipillas – Puffed fried bread you fill with honey.

Stake It Out – To watch without being seen.

Stone Lions – In Bandelier are two life-size crouching mountain lion statues carved side by side out of the soft bedrock. (A Guide to Bandelier National Monument)

Taps – Written in 1835. A bugle call played at dusk, during flag ceremonies, and at military funerals by the United States armed forces. It is also performed often at Boy Scout, Girl Scout, and Girl Guide meetings and camps at "lights out" (bedtime). (Wikipedia)

Tent Rocks – Tall, thin spires of rock. On top sits a hard rock. The softer rock on the bottom then erodes and gives it a cone shape.

Topo – Is short for Topographical Map; maps that depict in detail ground relief (landforms and terrain), drainage (lakes and rivers), forest cover, administrative areas, populated areas, transportation routes and facilities including roads and railways) and other manmade features.

Varmint – *Slang* – A troublesome wild animal, usually considered a problem (example: rats, mice, skunks.)

Notes

Chapter 1

[1] Tent Rock Ranch – Bob Marten, News Article, (KRQE Television, July 2011)

[2] Cochiti Pueblo – Lance Chilton, Katherine Chilton, Polly E. Arango, James Dudley, Nancy Neary, Patricia Stelzner, *New Mexico a New Guide to the Colorful State*, (University of New Mexico Press, 1991, p. 216)

[3] Valles Caldera – William deBuys, Don J. Unser, *Valles Caldera: A Vision for New Mexico's National Preserve,* (University of New Mexico Press, 2009)

[4] Bland – Marc Simmons, *The Town of Bland*, (Santa Fe Always on Line, Inc. 2000-2013)

[5] Bernalillo Mercantile Company – Lance Chilton, Katherine Chilton, Polly E. Arango, James Dudley, Nancy Neary, Patricia Stelzner, *New Mexico a New Guide to the Colorful State*, (University of New Mexico Press, 1991, p 229)

[6] Young's Apple Orchard – Lance Chilton, Katherine Chilton, Polly E. Arango, James Dudley, Nancy Neary, Patricia Stelzner, *New Mexico* a New *Guide to the Colorful State*, (University of New Mexico Press, 1991, p. 215)

[7] Dragon – *Drake's Comprehensive Compendium of Dragonology,* (Candlewick Press, 2010)

Chapter 2

[8] Boy Scouts –The Boy Scouts of America, *Handbook for Boys,* (Boys Scouts of America Press, 1937)

[9] Ravens – Bernd Heinrich, *Mind of the Raven,* (Harper Collins Publishers 2006)

Chapter 4

[10] Effie Jinks – Marc Simmons, *The Town of Bland*, (Santa Fe Always on Line, Inc., 2000-2013)

Chapter 5

[11] Bandelier National Monument – Dorothy Hoard, *A Guide to Bandelier National Monument,* (Los Alamos Historical Society, 1983)

Chapter 10

[12] Valle Grande – Craig Martin, *Valle Grande A History of the Baca Location No.* 1 (All Seasons Publishing, 2003)

[13] Los Alamos Ranch School – John D. Wirth and Linda Harvey Aldrich, *Los Alamos the Ranch School Years 1917 - 1943* (University of New Mexico Press, 2003)

Chapter 12

[14] San Antonio Hot Springs – Matt C. Bischoff, *Touring the New Mexico Hot Springs* (Morris Book Publishing, LLC; 2nd edition, 2008, p. 79)

Chapter 13

[15] Chili Line – David F. Myrick, *New Mexico's Railroads: A Historical Survey* (University Press, 1999, p. 117)

Chapter 14

[16] Robert Oppenheimer (Oppie) – Robert F. Bacher, *Robert Oppenheimer 1904 – 1967.* (Los Alamos Historical Society of Los Alamos, New Mexico, 1999, p 7)

Chapter 15

[17] Benceslado (Bences) Gonzales – John D. Wirth and Linda Harvey Aldrich, *Los Alamos The Ranch School Years 1917 - 1943* (University of New Mexico Press, 2003, p. 37)

The Tent Rocks in Pines Canyon, 2018

A Little Bit of Fran's Personal History and a Few Updates

When Fran came to Los Alamos in 1968, the first thing her husband and she did was to buy a Jeep to explore the beautiful mountains surrounding the town. They spent many of those first few years bouncing up and down many mountain dirt roads. On one of their road trips, when they were on the del Norte Canyon road, they passed the road that went to the ghost town of Bland. There was a large gate across the road. An old woman, whom Fran later found out was Effie Jinks, stood there holding a gun. They were trying to go to the ghost town Albemarle the next canyon over, but Effie wouldn't let them take that road. At the end of many dirt roads in the Jemez Mountains, they were more likely than not to meet a local character. Many people owned pockets of property in the Santa Fe National forest area, so when two of the biggest fires in the Jemez Mountains came along, they affected many people.

The Cerro Grande fire in 2000 burned along the West side of the town of Los Alamos and destroyed 400 homes. But because of the scar the Cerro Grande fire created, the next fire that happened in 2011, the Las Conchas fire, did not destroy any more of the Los Alamos/White Rock property.

The Las Conchas fire burned in the Jemez Mountains and destroyed many of the places Fran talks about in her book. The Dixon (previously Young's) Apple Orchard, the Tent Rock Guest Ranch, and the ghost town of Bland were all victims of this massive fire that burned over 1,500,000 acres of forest. It started on June 26, 2011, and burned for five days. This largest wildfire in New Mexico started when a tree blew down and hit a power line on the edge of the Valle Grande. The fire blew westward burning a large chunk of Bandelier National Monument, missing most of the Valles Caldera, and then turning north towards Los Alamos. The town of Los Alamos was again evacuated but nothing burned down during this fire.

112

In 2000, just before the Cerro Grande fire, Fran and her husband bought a small summer home on the top of Cochiti Mesa in the Jemez Mountains. They had a well for water, solar power for electricity, and a wood stove for heat. She no longer owned the place when the second fire took this cabin in the 2011 fire.

About 1.25 million years ago, a spectacular volcanic eruption created the 13-mile wide circular depression now known as the Valles Caldera. The Valles Caldera was privately owned for many years and you could drive by the south side of it on a public highway. It is a beautiful and inspiring landscape with great meadows. In 2000, the 95,000 acres were sold to the US government and a large chunk of it became the Valles Caldera Preserve. It is exciting to drive into it today.

Fran wrote "The Secret Dragons." The story of Bow and the three kids who cared for him took on a life of its own. Putting the story in a setting Fran was familiar with, where she had experienced her own mountain adventures, lived in her own cabin, and traveled many bumpy dirt roads, seemed like a natural setting for her tale. Fran will always miss the places in the Jemez she experienced and used for many of the settings for "The Secret Dragons," but because of the Valles Caldera Preserve, there are still many more places to explore in the Jemez Mountains.

Fran hopes you will enjoy the story of Bow and getting him back to his dragon parents, as well as the beautiful and ever enchanting mountain surroundings here in Northern New Mexico.

Annie Kuiper - Editor

Made in the USA
Lexington, KY
19 November 2019